Love Bites

by

Jo Cotterill

Illustrated by Astrid Jaekel

For Patience Thomson

First published in 2012 in Great Britain by
Barrington Stoke Ltd
18 Walker St, Edinburgh, EH3 7LP

www.barringtonstoke.co.uk

ISBN: 978-1-78112-001-9

Printed in China by Leo

Contents

Chapter 1
Tick Tock

Tara smoothed her long golden hair. "If you tell him, you'll have to kill him," she said.

I gave her a look. "I'm not going to tell him."

"He's got under your skin," she said. "He's a danger to both of us."

I felt my face go red. "James isn't a danger. He doesn't know, so he can't tell."

Tara gave a sigh. "I know you like him, Grace, but he's not one of us. You've got too close."

I turned away from her. I could hear the clock tick in the hall.

Tick ... tock ...

"It's not like that," I said.

"Yes it is," she said. "I can see it in your eyes. You love him. And one day soon, you'll tell him."

The garden outside our window was full of flowers. Blue, white, pink, green ... as I looked at them my eyes filled with tears and I blinked.

I didn't know what to say. Tara wasn't my sister but I told people she was. And she was right. I *did* love James. And I *was* too close. James knew a lot about me. But he didn't know what I was.

Not yet.

Chapter 2
A Trip with James

"Hey." James gave me a smile. *The* smile. The one that made me feel weak. If my heart still worked, it would skip a beat for him.

I smiled back. "Hey, yourself."

He put his strong arms around me.
"I've had an idea. Can we go away this
weekend?"

"What?" My head was fuzzy.
"Where?"

"Anywhere. I just want to be with
you." He looked into my eyes. His eyes
were blue, the blue of a summer sky.
I swear if I looked deep into them, I
could see the sun. The sun like I
remember it, when I could stand in its
rays and feel its heat.

"What about your parents?" I asked.

"I told them I was staying over with a mate," he said. "Come away with me. Please?" He leaned over and kissed me.

It was like my mind was melting. His lips were soft and warm. I couldn't see, couldn't hear. There was only James. I didn't care what Tara said. She wasn't my mother. She didn't know what was best for me.

I opened my eyes and smiled at James. "Yes," I said.

****

We got on a bus. James had a tent with
him. I don't like camping much, but I didn't
care. I would go anywhere with James.

I had left a note for Tara:

Gone away for weekend. Stuff to do.

She'd guess I was with James. But by the time she saw the note, we'd have gone.

I snuggled into James's side. His dark hair flopped down over his face as he looked at me. "You're amazing, Grace, you know?" he said. "I'm just crazy about you."

I smiled at him. "Me too. You're the first boyfriend I've ever really ... er."
I stopped.

He looked puzzled. "I'm the first boyfriend you've what?"

Oh dear. I was supposed to be 15, wasn't I? I had almost started to talk about my life! Big mistake, Grace!

"You're the first *boy* I've really liked," I said in a hurry. *I'm only 15*, I told myself. *I can't tell him about the other boyfriends, the ones I've had over the past 50 years.*

He smiled and kissed me. We almost missed our stop.

I've lived a long time. Not as long as Tara, but a lot longer than James. I'd had other boyfriends. But somehow he was different.

He was so *good*. So nice, and kind and sweet.

When I was with him I could see what my own life was missing.

Chapter 3
The Truth

When we got off the bus, James pulled out a map. "This way," he said.

"What, no sat nav?" I said, as a joke.

He smiled. "No, I'm doing it like they did in the old days. Come on, it's a mile down this road."

"Where are we going?" I asked.

"You'll see when we get there." He took my hand, and again I felt that rush of *sweetness*. What was happening to me? In the past, a good feeling like that would have made me feel sick. But now ... now I wanted it, wished for it.

The camp site was a field. "This is it?" I said, feeling a bit let down.

"Over here." James led me across the field. It was a cloudy day but dry and warm, and the place was full of wild flowers. We were the only ones there. At the far end, the ground went down a slope, and all of a sudden ...

I gasped. "The sea!" It was there below us, calm and flat as a mirror. There were two tiny boats far out, but nothing else – nothing but flowers and the sea, all that way below us.

"Careful!" James grabbed my hand. "Don't go too near."

"How come there isn't a fence?" I asked, as I looked around. "You could fall off the edge!"

"I dunno," he said. "It's private land."

"Private land?" I raised my eyebrows. "So we're not supposed to be here?"

He looked into my eyes. "Is that a problem?"

"No ..." My words dried up. The only thing I cared about was that I was here, with him.

We ate chicken stew from a packet, heated over a little stove. James had put up our tent and we could see the sea from the door flap. "This is perfect," I said with a sigh. "Just being with you ... I feel like I've never felt before."

He put an arm around me. "Me too."

I *wanted* to tell him. He deserved to hear the truth, didn't he? I moved to face him. "I want to tell you something," I said.

"You can tell me anything," he said.

"I know." I stopped for a moment to think. Was this really the right thing to do? After I had told him, what would he think of me? But I was sick of pretending to be something I wasn't. James was good – he would understand.

I took a deep breath. "Promise me you won't freak out."

He gave me a funny look. "What do you mean?"

"No matter what I tell you," I said, "promise me you won't freak out."

He started to smile but then he saw my face. "OK," he said. "I promise. But I'm sure it can't be that bad."

I took his hand in mine. "You know how you always say I feel cold?"

"Yeah. You need to wear more clothes."

"It's not that." I put his hand over my heart – the heart that had stopped beating over 50 years ago. "Feel," I said.

He was puzzled. "Feel what?"

"Can you feel my heart beating?"

"Um ..." He waited for a moment, then moved his hand a bit to the right. "Hang on a sec."

"Try my neck," I said. I lifted my chin so that he could feel for the pulse in my neck.

He touched my skin, making me shiver. I felt his fingers move from one spot to another as he looked for something that wasn't there. "That's weird," he said.

I took his hand again. "It's not weird. It's not there."

"What do you mean?"

I looked deep into his eyes. "I don't have a pulse. My heart doesn't beat."

"What are you talking about?" he said. "Of course it does! If it didn't, you wouldn't be alive."

"I'm not alive," I said.

He didn't understand.

"I'm undead," I told him. "I'm a vampire."

Chapter 4
You Want My Blood!

He laughed. Then he said, "This is a joke, right?"

"No," I said. "No, it isn't. I'm a vampire. I was born in 1943, just before the war ended. When I was 15, I ran away from home. Tara found me. She was kind and looked after me. I didn't know what she was, until it was too late. But I don't blame her for changing me. She wanted a friend. She'd been on her own for years."

James still didn't get it.

"I'm a vampire," I said again, louder this time. "I've been a vampire for over 50 years."

"You don't have pointy teeth," he said.

"Not until I need to feed," I said, and then stopped. That was something I didn't want to talk about at all.

"Feed?" he said. He pulled away his hand. "Feed on what?"

"James ..."

"No, this is just stupid," he said. "You're talking rubbish. Vampires are ... They're not real."

I said nothing.

"Besides, you don't burn up in the sun," he said. "I mean, you do go out in the sun, don't you?"

I shook my head. "No. If the sun's out, I wear my big hat. You know, the one you said looked like a dinner plate."

"What about garlic?"

I screwed up my nose. "What about it? It's yuck."

"Let me look for your pulse again," he said. "I'll find it."

"All right." I lay back on the grass. "If that's the only thing that will prove it to you. Go on."

He felt my wrists, my neck – he put his ear on my chest. I shivered at his touch.

I love him, I thought, as I looked up at the sky. *I love him so much. I was right to tell him.*

With every moment that passed, James became more panicked. "You have to have a pulse," he kept saying. "You have to!"

I lay back and waited.

In the end, he sat up. There was something new in his eyes. "You don't have a heart-beat," he said, and his voice shook. "You ... There's nothing there."

"James," I said, "listen ..."

"No." He got to his feet and backed away. "What *are* you?"

"I told you." I stood up too. "James, I didn't want to lie to you. I – I love you."

"You *love* me? How can you love me if – if you don't have a heart?"

That hurt. I felt tears in my eyes. "James, it's not about blood ..."

I had said the wrong thing. All of a sudden, he was terrified.

"Blood!" he said. His hands went to his neck. "You want my blood!"

"No!" I cried. "No, James! I could never do that!"

"Is that why you said yes to this camping trip?" He looked around in a wild way, like he was planning to run. "So you could *bite* me? No one knows where we are! *Jeez!*"

I took a step closer, and my foot knocked the little stove over. Hot water splashed onto my leg.

"Ouch!" I yelled. "James, you have to listen to me. I said yes to the trip because I want to be with you. Because after 50 years, I found someone I want to be with – you!"

"I have to get out of here," he said. "I can't look at you. I can't be with you. You can't be real."

"Please!" I called. Tears spilled down my face. "James, just wait!"

But he had started to run across the field, back to the road. Without thinking, I ran after him.

He was faster than me. I knew I could never catch him, but still I ran, hoping that somehow he would change his mind.

There was someone at the other end of the field. Because of the tears, I couldn't see who it was, but it looked like the person was running to meet us – to meet James. It was another girl, wasn't it?

I rubbed my eyes, and then I gasped.

The girl running towards James was Tara.

Chapter 5
Save James!

I was too far away to hear what Tara
said, but James stopped. He stopped dead,
like he'd run into a wall. Then he started to
walk backwards, away from Tara.

Slowly, she pushed him towards me. I
watched them get closer and closer. By the

time they got to me, James's face was almost as white as my own.

"Hello, Grace," said Tara in a sweet voice. "How lovely to see you."

I was angry. "You followed me," I said.

"Of course I did, darling," Tara said. She swished her golden hair. "I was worried about you. I knew you would tell him. And you did, didn't you?" She looked at James.

"You're another one!" he gasped.

"Tara is my sire," I said. "She made me into a vampire."

James gulped. "And you're both going to kill me now."

"No!" I said, just as Tara said, "Yes!"

"No," I said, louder. "We are not going to kill him."

Tara gave me a cold look. "We can't let him live. He's a danger to us."

"I won't let you," I said.

Her eyes opened wide. "*What* did you say?"

"I won't let you kill him," I said. "I love him." I turned to James. "I love you," I said. "I know you don't believe me, but it's true."

The light was fading over the sea, and the sky was getting dark. James's face was pale. "Look out!" he cried.

It all happened so fast. From behind me, Tara leaped and landed on my back, knocking me to the ground. My face smashed into the grass. Then I felt her jump off me. I scrambled to my feet.

Tara had James by the neck, hissing in his face. "You men, you think you can come between us. But you can't!"

"Tara, let him go!" I rushed forward, but she batted me away as if I was a fly.

"It's too late," she said. "But he looks kind of tasty ..."

James tried to scream as Tara opened her mouth and her teeth grew into sharp points.

"NO!" I yelled, leaping on to her, dragging her away from James. She fell back on top of me. We were moving so fast that she rolled right over my head.

I sprang to my feet, putting myself in front of James. "You will NOT hurt him!" I screamed.

Tara got to her feet, about to say something. But the look on her face changed, and she wobbled. She looked down ...

And then she fell, into the air, over the edge of the cliff ...

Chapter 6
After the End

James grabbed my arm as I stepped forwards. "Don't!" he said. "You'll fall too!"

"But I have to see!" I shouted. I pulled free and got down on the grass, crawling to the edge.

Tara's body was nowhere to be seen, and the sea was as smooth as glass.

I was panting. "But she – she can't be gone ... Oh No! Tara!" The tears ran down my face again. I knew it was stupid. She'd tried to kill the boy I loved! But she'd beenmy best friend for over 50 years and I loved her too.

"Where did she go?" James was panting too.

"Down there," I sobbed. "Into the sea."

"But she's a vam ... She can't die like that," he said. "Can she?"

"I don't know," I said. "But she can be hurt. Hurt so much that she ..." I stopped. "She'll take a long time to heal."

"How long?" he asked.

I turned to look at him. "A year maybe."

He looked into my eyes. "You saved my life."

"I'd do anything for you," I said, my voice soft. "I love you."

After a moment, he stood up. "Grace, I need some time."

I got up too. "I know. And I've got time. Take as long as you need." It hurt me to say it. All I wanted was to rush into his arms, but he was still afraid. "I'll wait for you, James."

He nodded, his gaze never leaving mine. Then he turned and started packing up the tent.

"Are you going to head home now?" I asked. "It's night."

"I can't stay here," he said. "You understand."

And I did. So I helped him pack up the camping stuff, and I walked with him across the field to the road. And then I said goodbye, and he walked away.

I watched him until I could no longer see him in the dark. And then I went back to the edge of the cliff and looked over.

How long would it be before Tara came back? I didn't know.

I didn't know if I would be with James by then, but I hoped so. Somewhere far away from here, where Tara couldn't find us. Because if she ever did ...

I shivered. Then I turned to go home, to the empty cottage with the flowers in the garden and the sound of time passing from the clock in the hall.

Our books are tested
for children and young people by
children and young people.

Thanks to everyone who consulted on
a manuscript for their time and effort in
helping us to make our books better
for our readers.